Muhlenberg County Public Libraries
108 E. Broad Street
Central City, KY 42330

GEENIE

AND THE Weenie Race

E
CC 0373
$ 17·00
2/13

Amy Caetta and Karen Lomheim

© 2012 Amy Caetta and Karen Lomheim
All rights reserved
ISBN 978-0-615-65530-7

Editing by Author One Stop (www.AuthorOneStop.com)

Interior and cover design and production
by Joanne Shwed, Backspace Ink (www.backspaceink.com)

Illustrations by Gabhor Utomo

To order copies, please visit our website at geenietheweenie.com

doxieracer@geenietheweenie.com
www.geenietheweenie.com
www.facebook.com/GeenieAndTheWeenieRace

This book is dedicated to Presley,
the real-life inspiration behind this story,
our families, and all who adore Dachshunds.

Geenie was so excited that she could barely stop her tail from wagging!

Today was adoption day at Sandy Dunes Doxie Rescue, a shelter for miniature Dachshunds.

Geenie's new owners—Sydney, her younger brother Sam, and their parents—were due to arrive at any moment to take Geenie to her new home.

Geenie waited for her new family by the front gate.

When Geenie caught sight of them, she playfully zipped around the yard like a race car on a track!

Sydney and Sam were delighted to see Geenie, too.

They chased her as she darted across the yard and were amazed how her pint-sized legs moved so quickly.

A rescue volunteer suggested that they enter Geenie in the upcoming Doxie Dash beach race. Sydney giggled aloud as she imagined how funny it would be to watch a bunch of short-legged little Dachshunds race against each other!

Sam asked Mom if they could enter Geenie in the race. "I think that's a great idea, but Geenie will need some training."

"Sam and I will be her coaches," Sydney proudly stated.

Dad mentioned that, since the Doxie Dash was quickly approaching, they should begin Geenie's training right away. Sydney and Sam already liked Geenie and knew that they were going to make a good team.

Sydney and Sam began training Geenie for the Doxie Dash the next day.

They worked tirelessly, making a starting gate out of a cardboard box.

Sam carefully placed Geenie in the box.

When Sam opened the flap, Geenie took off like a slingshot!

She was eager to get to Sydney, who waited for her with yummy dog treats at the opposite end of the backyard.

Sydney and Sam chased Geenie at the park playground so she could get used to running in sand.

Geenie's bitty legs kicked up the sand behind her as she sprinted around the playground.

Sydney and Sam thought it would be fun to wear matching t-shirts at the race to show their enthusiasm.

They designed a "Team Geenie" logo for the shirts, featuring their favorite colors: lavender and blue.

The day of the Doxie Dash arrived.

It was a lovely day at the beach. The sky was crystal clear and Sam knew that Geenie was ready for the big race.

Sydney was a bit nervous.

After all, this was Geenie's first race!

Sydney and Sam noticed all sorts of Dachshunds that entered in the race.

There were long- and short-haired Dachshunds, spotted Dachshunds—even copper-coated Dachshunds, just like Geenie.

Mom and Dad, wearing their Team Geenie t-shirts, set up their beach chairs in the crowd of race fans.

Sydney and Sam waited with Geenie by the starting gate.

When the announcer declared that it was time to begin the Doxie Dash, Sam walked Geenie to the starting gate.

They took their places alongside the other racer Dachshunds and their coaches. Sydney skipped on the beach to wait for Geenie at the finish line.

The announcer said each Dachshund's name: "In Lane 1, Brutus. In Lane 2, Geenie …" Mom and Dad cheered when they heard Geenie's name.

After the announcer called all of the names, he shouted, "On your mark, get set, go!"

The gate was lifted and the Dachshunds were off!

Their quick, teeny legs made the sand fly in the air behind them as they scurried across the seashore. The fans were so excited!

Geenie whisked past several Dachshunds on her way to the finish line.

Then, Geenie suddenly slowed her pace, shook her head, and blinked her eyes.

"Oh, no!" thought Sydney. "She has sand in her eyes!"

Sydney hollered from the finish line, "Come on, Geenie! You can do it, girl!"

She loudly shook the little bag of dog treats in her hand, hoping that Geenie would hear.

Geenie heard the yummy
treats shaking in the bag,
increased her pace, and bolted
past the other Dachshunds.

She took the lead by a nose
and crossed the finish line
into Sydney's arms!

Geenie gulped her treats
and licked Sydney's face.

Sam rushed to join them at
the finish line and gave Geenie a big hug!

They were proud of their racer Dachshund.

Mom and Dad were proud of Geenie's coaches.

The announcer declared Geenie the winner of the Doxie Dash and congratulated Sydney and Sam.

The first prize was a day of pampering at a dog spa and an appearance as an honorary guest in the Summer Celebration Parade!

Sydney and Sam told the story of Geenie's adoption to a local reporter, who was covering the race.

The reporter snapped a picture of them holding their little champion.

The next day, the newspaper's headline read:

"A Rescue Doxie
with Moxie
Wins the Dash!"

At the Summer Celebration Parade, Sam sat next to Sydney in a shimmering red convertible and held Geenie on his lap.

Geenie's ears perked up as she curiously glanced at the merriment around her.

Sydney and Sam, proudly wearing Team Geenie t-shirts, waved as they passed the spectators.

Marching band tunes filled the air and clowns on stilts amused the parade watchers.

Sydney leaned over, scratched Geenie behind her ears, and turned to Sam.

"We make a good team!"

Sam smiled, looked at his sister and then at Geenie,
and replied, "We make an awesome team!"
Geenie barked in agreement.